THIS MOON-TASTIC
STORYBOOK
BELONGS TO

....

....

Super Moon Adventure

Night in the city. The PJ Masks were ready to stop fiendish villains from messing with your day . . .

"Whoa!" shouted Catboy. "Look at the sky."

Up above them, the Moon shone full and bright.

"That's the Harvest Moon," said Gekko. "It only happens once a year."

"It's so cool!" gasped Owlette.

Suddenly a figure blocked the heroes' view. Luna Girl!

"Check out my Luna Magnet," she cried. "The Harvest Moon has supercharged it."

"What are you talking about?" asked Owlette.

"I'm going to the Moon," cackled Luna Girl.

"And when I get my hands on the Harvest Moon Crystal, my powers are going to be unstoppable!"

The PJ Masks raced back to their HQ. Their little metal helper, PJ Robot, was waiting inside.

"We've got to stop Luna Girl before she gets the Moon Crystal," said Catboy.

"Really?" gasped Gekko.

"Yes," replied Owlette. "I've always wanted to go into space!"

Gekko was not so sure.

Catboy switched the totem pole HQ into its super-cool rocket mode.
"Thirty seconds to blast off, " he said. "To your stations, everyone!"

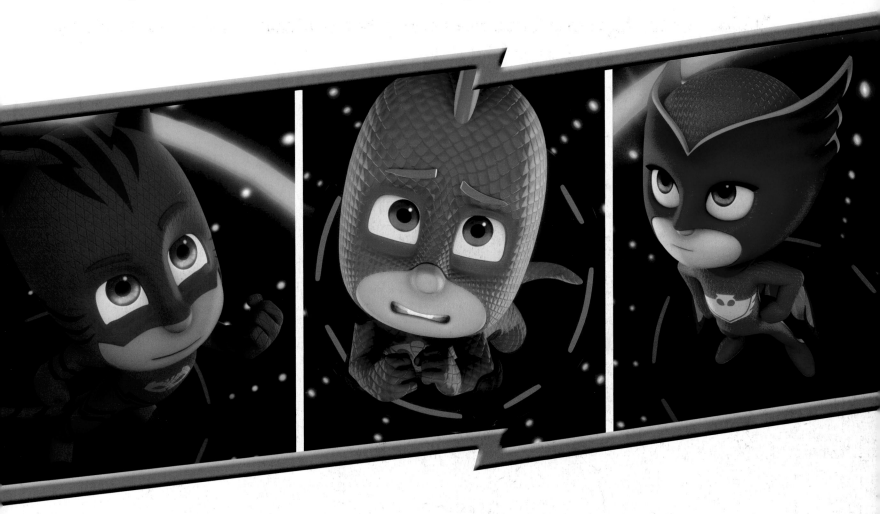

PJ Robot took over the controls. The heroes ran to their elevators,
then zoomed up to the flight deck.

"Three . . . two . . . one . . . blast off!"

The HQ roared into the air and began to change into a space rocket!

"Next stop, the Moon," said Catboy.

"What if Luna Girl is bluffing?" said Gekko. "We're leaving the whole
city unprotected."

But the PJ Masks' course was set – the heroes were racing to the Moon!

Luna Girl whooshed through the sky in her Luna Bubble. She spotted the PJ Masks roaring behind her and scowled.

"A totem pole rocket ship?" she bellowed. "Oh no you don't! You are not going to spoil my big moment."

The villain held up her Luna Magnet.

Boom! Boom! Boom!

Energy bubbles blasted towards the PJ Masks' ship.

"Luna Girl's trying to throw us off-course," said Catboy. "We've got to dodge those bubbles."

"I'll handle this," answered Owlette. "Hold on!"

Owlette steered the rocket left and right, zigzagging past the energy bubbles.

"Look out!" bleeped PJ Robot.

Another blast of bubbles came rushing through the sky. Owlette tried to steer out of their way, but this time they were just too fast.

"Sorry guys," she said. "I couldn't dodge them."

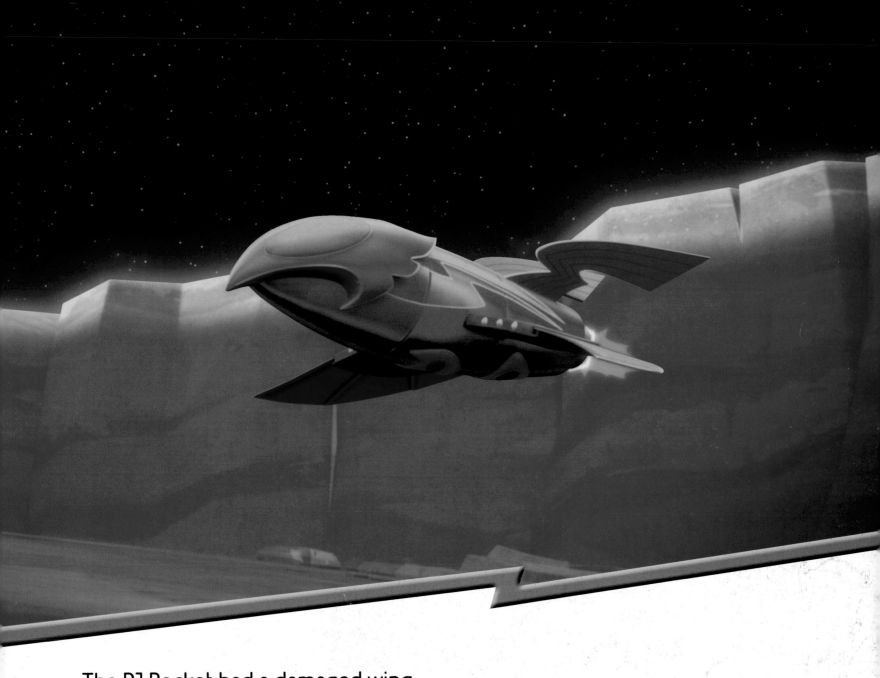

The PJ Rocket had a damaged wing.

"Can we fix it?" asked Gekko. "How will we get back home?"

Owlette didn't answer. She was busy trying to land on the Moon.

"This is going to get a little bumpy," she warned.

The PJ Masks landed with a noisy thud.

"Phew!" said Gekko. "I'm glad that's over."

The heroes spotted Luna Girl. Something seemed to be pulling her through the air.

"I don't like the look of this," exclaimed Catboy. "We're going after her."

Gekko hung back. He had never been this far away from home before.

"I'm scared that we're going to get stuck here," he whispered.

"I understand," smiled Owlette. "That's how I felt on my first sleepover."

Catboy had an idea. He asked Gekko to stay and guard the ship,

while PJ Robot worked on the repairs.

"You got it!" said Gekko, relieved.

Catboy and Owlette went to grab their space suits.

"To the PJ Rovers!"

A few seconds later, the ship opened its landing door.

"Activating PJ Rovers!"

Catboy and Owlette zoomed down the ramp onto the surface of the Moon. Their bikes skidded across the lunar landscape.

Catboy pressed a button on his space suit. "Switching on helmet communications. Do you read me, Gekko?"

The hero popped up on Gekko's radar screen.

"Hey!" he cried. "Now I can see everything you're seeing. Cool!"

"Keep an eye out for us, Gekko," nodded Catboy.

Owlette found Luna Girl with her Owl Eyes.

"She's in that crater," she cried. "We'd better hurry."

Luna Girl's Luna Magnet had pulled her towards the Moon Crystal!

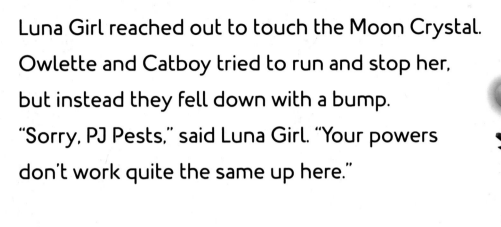

Luna Girl reached out to touch the Moon Crystal. Owlette and Catboy tried to run and stop her, but instead they fell down with a bump. "Sorry, PJ Pests," said Luna Girl. "Your powers don't work quite the same up here."

Purple light filled the crater. The Moon Crystal floated towards Luna Girl's magnet, turning it into a powerful Luna Wand.

Luna Girl banged the wand on the ground. Giant crystals appeared
out of nowhere, rising up to form a huge Lunar Fortress.
"Ha ha!" cried the villain, disappearing inside.
Owlette and Catboy went in after her.

Catboy and Owlette tiptoed into Luna Girl's lair.

"Shh," whispered Catboy. The heroes had to be careful to stay
out of sight . . .

Luna Girl swooped into view. She had been watching them the whole time! The baddie pointed her Luna Wand at the heroes.

"Gotcha!" she screeched.

Two crystal cages burst out of the floor, trapping the PJs inside.

Owlette spoke into her helmet communicator.

"Gekko! Do you read me?"

"Where's lizard boy?" screeched Luna Girl.

"You'll never find him," said Catboy.

Luna Girl smirked. Her wand would track him down. And when it did he would be sorry he ever came to the Moon!

Back inside the ship, Gekko stayed by his computer. He could see and hear everything.

"Thanks to this Moon Crystal, my powers are stronger than ever!" Luna Girl cried gleefully. Gekko leapt up. The heroes were in trouble!

Gekko wanted to go and help his friends, but he felt scared, too.

"Is it safe out there?" he wondered. "What if I float away?"

PJ Robot pointed to the hero's space suit and special moon boots.

"You're right," nodded Gekko. "I can do this!"

It was time to be a hero. Gekko got into his space suit, then revved up his PJ Rover. Soon he was riding towards the crystal fortress.

"Super Gekko Camouflage!"

Gekko crawled inside the fortress. He clung to a wall high up in the shadows, trying to stay out of sight.

Down below, Luna Girl waved her wand. Now she had worked out the power of the Moon Crystal, she was starting to make plans.

"Imagine if I forced everyone you know to be my loyal subjects here on the Moon, forever," she declared.

"You wouldn't!" shouted Owlette.

Luna Girl grinned. "Who's going to stop me?"

Gekko took his chance. But when he crawled down to free his friends, Luna Girl zapped him with her Luna Wand.

"Look who's here," she gloated.

Poor Gekko. Now he was trapped as well!

Luna Girl waved at the PJ prisoners.

"I'm going to Earth to collect my loyal subjects," she announced. "Bye-bye!"

The PJ Masks felt glum. The world was in danger and there was nothing they could do about it . . . or was there?

"I have an idea," said Catboy. **"Super Cat Speed!"**

The hero raced around his cage. It began to shudder and shake.

"You're going to crack the crystals!" gasped Owlette.

Gekko pushed his cage closer to the others. **"Super Gekko Muscles!"**
Now all the crystals were cracking!

Out in space, Luna Girl felt herself being pulled back towards the fortress. "It can't be," she muttered. "There's no way those PJ Pests got out." Wrong! The PJ Masks were free.

"We've got to get back to Earth," shouted Catboy.

PJ Robot beeped into the helmet communicator. The ship was ready to go!

Luna Girl burst into the fortress, blasting her wand at the PJ Masks.

"Quick!" cried Catboy. "Run!"

"That won't help you!" smirked the villain.

"We've got to do something," decided Owlette. "Let's split up!"
The PJ Masks headed in different directions. Once they were apart, it was easier to get out of the baddie's way.

But Luna Girl managed to corner Gekko.
The hero braced himself. **"Super Gekko Shield!"**
Luna Girl zapped, but the blast bounced off Gekko's force field. She dropped the wand – and Owlette was there just in time to catch it!

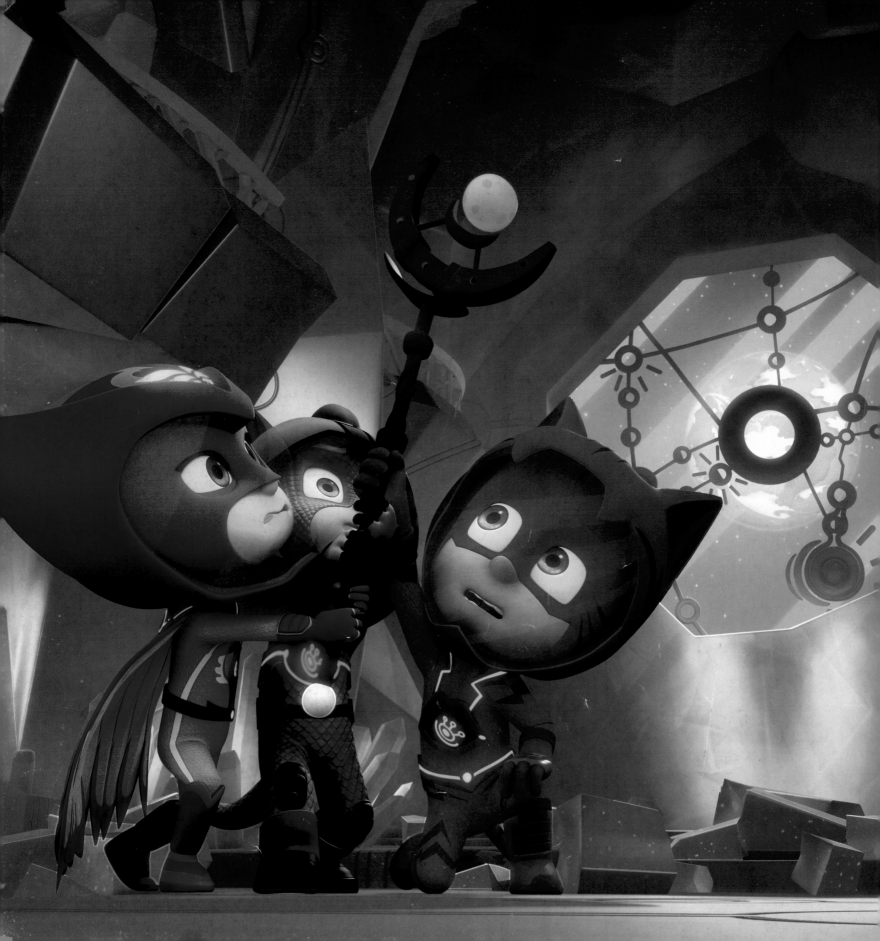

Owlette felt the Luna Wand pulling against her. Gekko and Catboy rushed to help.

"It only responds to me," said Luna Girl. "Luna Wand, blast those pesky PJs to pieces!"

The Luna Wand tried to obey. The PJ Masks were dragged up and down, and left and right! But instead of blasting at them, energy bolts darted all around the chamber.

"Noooo!" shouted Luna Girl. "You're ruining my fortress."

The Luna Wand gave one last blast. The force was so powerful, it knocked the Harvest Moon Crystal onto the floor!

"I'll take that!" said Owlette, catching it in her hand.

Luna Girl's power was drained. It was time to go home.

"To the Rovers!" cried Catboy.

"Hooray!" cheered Gekko.

The PJ Masks soared back to Earth. As soon as they landed, the totem pole changed back into the HQ again.

"Home sweet home!" beamed Gekko.

Owlette held up the Harvest Moon Crystal.

"Let's put it in HQ's vault," decided Catboy. "It will be safe there."

Gekko smiled at his friends.

"You were really brave out there," said Owlette.

"It was a little scary at first," he replied, "but being heroes together made everything OK."

"And we stopped Luna Girl!" cheered Catboy.

Right on cue, the baddie appeared.

"You win this time, PJ Pests," she grumbled, "but that Moon Crystal will be mine again!"

The PJ Masks smiled. They weren't so sure about that!

PJ MASKS ALL SHOUT HOORAY,
'CAUSE IN THE NIGHT WE SAVED THE DAY!